KT-450-733

For my gentle snowflake Lila

First published 2013 by Macmillan Children's Books
This edition published 2014 by Macmillan Children's Books
a division of Macmillan Publishers Limited
20 New Wharf Road, London N1 9RR
Basingstoke and Oxford
Associated companies throughout the world
www.panmacmillan.com
ISBN: 978-1-4472-2015-2
Text and illustrations copyright © Natalie Russell 2013
Moral rights asserted. All rights reserved.
A CIP catalogue record for this book is available
from the British Library.
Printed in China
9 8 7 6 5 4 3 2 1

With special thanks
to Ailsa McWilliam
and Peacock Visual Arts

Natalie Russell

Rabbits in the Snow

a book of opposites

MACMILLAN CHILDREN'S BOOKS

Little Rabbit is making a snowman.
Her snowball is very **small**.

Brown Rabbit is helping.
His snowball is very **big**.

Look at Rose Rabbit skating on the pond.
She moves very **fast**!

Grey Rabbit is **slow**. The ice is so slippy!

Honey Rabbit is up on the hill.
Her basket is now **full**.

Rust Rabbit's sledge is **empty**.
So he offers her a ride!

All the way from the **top** . . .

wheeeeeeeee

eeeeeeeeeeeee

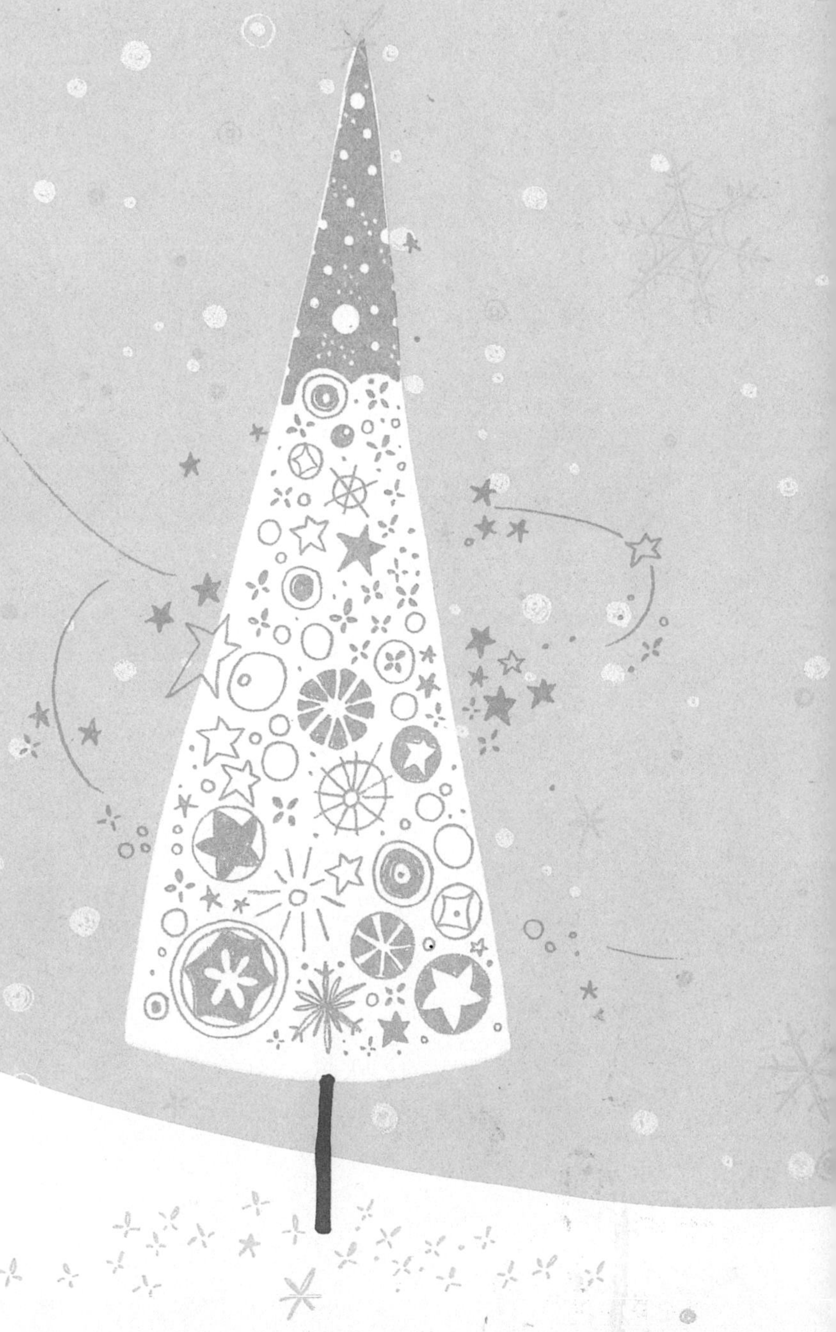

. . . to the **bottom**.

Where a snowman is waiting!

But he's not quite finished.
What does he need?

An **old** top hat.

A **new** scarf.

A pair of **soft**, fluffy earmuffs.

And a **hard**, crunchy carrot.

That's much better!

Goodbye **cold** snow!

Hello **hot** carrot soup!

Little Rabbit has made enough for everyone.